To Emily and Skye,
Best Wishes
Clive
2012

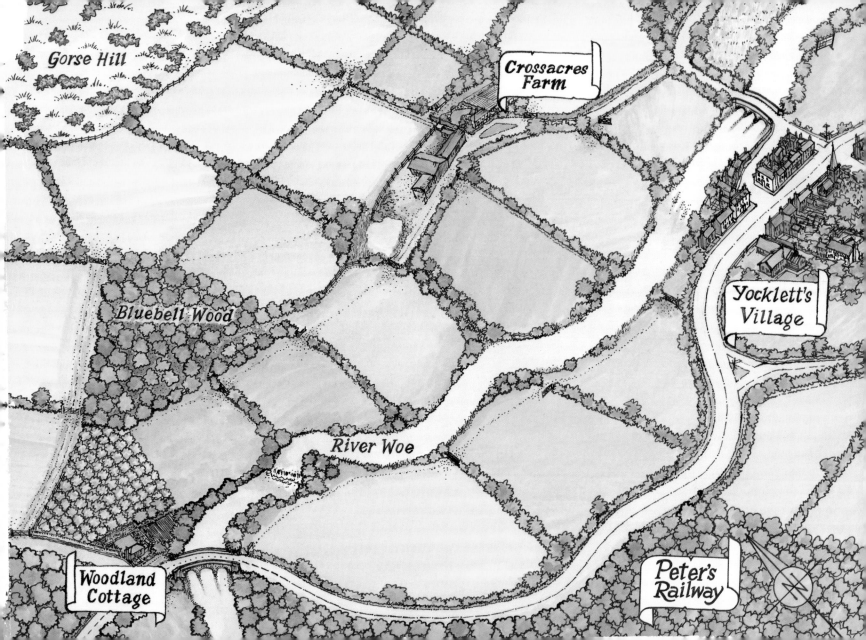

Peter's Railway 1

First edition 2008
First reprinted 2009
Revised edition 2011

Published by Christopher Vine 2008

Printed by The Amadeus Press
Cleckheaton, West Yorkshire,
England.

ISBN 978-0-9553359-1-4

Foreword

As someone who has spent most of his life involved with railways, be it working on them, preserving them or just enjoying them, I often wonder where the future engineers and enthusiasts will come from.

It is perfectly clear that young children love trains and railways and there is a huge selection of books for them. However after a certain age there is nothing to follow on and their interest can end.

This is where Peter's Railway comes in. Here is a book for train loving youngsters which will continue and develop their interest after they have grown out of the more junior books.

The story is great fun and realistic as Peter and his Grandpa set about building their own miniature steam railway across a farm. There is some simple engineering mixed in with the story which is unusual these days, however it is clearly explained and adds to the scope and charm of the book.

So much of life today is made up of activities which bring instant gratification and the much longer and slower pleasure of making things as a hobby or a job has been lost for most people. This book brings out the fun and sense of achievement in making something for yourself and I hope it will inspire youngsters to want to learn about how things work and see how interesting it can be.

I hope it will also encourage a future generation to get involved with a preserved railway or to make models themselves and possibly even consider a career in engineering.

Dr Pete Waterman, OBE

To my little family Peter, Harry, Kitty and Cato.

The watercolour story illustrations are by John Wardle

Before the Railway

Peter lives in a small house called Woodland Cottage. It is in the countryside with gently rolling hills, old woods and farms all around. It isn't a large house but it is in such a lovely location that he hopes he will live there all his life.

A few miles down the road is the small village where Peter goes to school. There are all the usual things you find in country villages: A green in the middle where they play cricket in the summer, a few shops, a pub and a small playground.

Living at Woodland Cottage with Peter are his Mum and Dad, Jo and Colin and the two baby twins, Kitty and Harry. Peter's Mum and Dad look after them all very well and are the sort of parents that every boy would wish for. There is always good food to eat, lots of fun things to do and plenty of lively talk and jokes.

The twins, being babies, don't do very much except make cute gurgling or cooing noises and some dreadful smells. (Peter knows he was the same only a few years ago but it doesn't make the smells any better.)

Across some fields and at the other side of Bluebell Wood, is Crossacres Farm where Peter's Grandma and Grandpa live. Grandpa Gerald has been a farmer nearly all his life. At his farm he keeps cows and sheep and also grows oats for the local horses. Grandma Pat is very good with the animals and is the most fantastic cook. There is never a day without fresh cakes for tea and she grows all her own fruit and vegetables at the bottom of the garden.

Keeping them company at the farm are Cato the cat and Minnie the dog. Cato is a funny cat with lovely dotty fur and a sort of double personality. He is either very lazy and sleeps all day on someone's bed (under a duvet), or he is going mad, chasing leaves around the garden and showing off how fast he can run.

Minnie is a Jack Russell who can smell biscuits at several hundred metres and loves long walks. Minnie also has very good hearing and can hear a biscuit tin being moved or opened even when she is outside, apparently asleep in the sun. She's a pretty little dog who is full of life and mischief, with wiry fur that sticks out at funny angles. She always likes to be in the middle of whatever is going on, with her tail wagging madly.

There are quite a few buildings at Crossacres Farm, what with the house, barns and dairy, but there is one place where Grandpa spends a lot of his time --- The Shed. He calls it his workshop but to everyone else it is The Shed.

Although Grandpa is very busy on the farm, there is nothing he likes better than to disappear into his workshop for hours at a time. Some people have a shed to keep hamsters or rabbits, others go into them to read and most people have a hut in the garden just to keep things in. Grandpa however, likes to make things in his shed.

Some of Peter's favourite toys came from Grandpa's workshop, including a model farm, a small roundabout for the garden and, best of all, a pedal go-kart.

Peter loves going into Grandpa's workshop. There is so much to see and there is always some new project which is not yet finished. Above all there is a unique smell; a mixture of old oils, machinery, cut wood and possibly a bit of Grandpa himself.

Now that Peter is getting older, he sometimes helps with the construction projects. The current one is a new wheel barrow for Grandma. It has two wheels at the front so that it does not tip over so easily.

Peter loves looking at all the tools in Grandpa's workshop. There are lots of hand tools, like hammers, screwdrivers, spanners and pliers. There is also a vice for clamping things while working on them. However his favourite tools are the special machines for making metal parts: The lathe, milling machine and the drill. When he

was tiny Grandpa used to hold him up so that he could see all the parts going round and round. Sometimes they would go very slowly so that he could see it all clearly. Other times Grandpa would make them go round so fast that there was only a whirring sound and the machines were just a blur of speed.

A Tricky Problem

Grandpa and Peter were both very happy people, but there was just one thing which was not perfect. They wished they could visit each other more often. It was about two miles along the winding road from the farm to Woodland Cottage and this was a bit too far to walk. There was always so much to do at the farm that Peter often wanted to go there after school. And Grandpa often wanted to go down to Woodland Cottage to see his young family.

Now most people would just get in their car and drive the short distance in a few minutes, but this was difficult for Grandpa because he didn't have one. In fact he hated cars and thought they were nasty, noisy contraptions which polluted his clean country air with all their smelly exhausts. Also he had noticed that almost everyone he saw in cars seemed to look cross and unhappy and often appeared rude and impatient. Grandpa was always cheerful and took his time over things.

Another way to travel between the farm and Woodland Cottage would be to go by bicycle. For Grandpa the problem was that he often wanted to go with Grandma but there was only one seat on his bike.

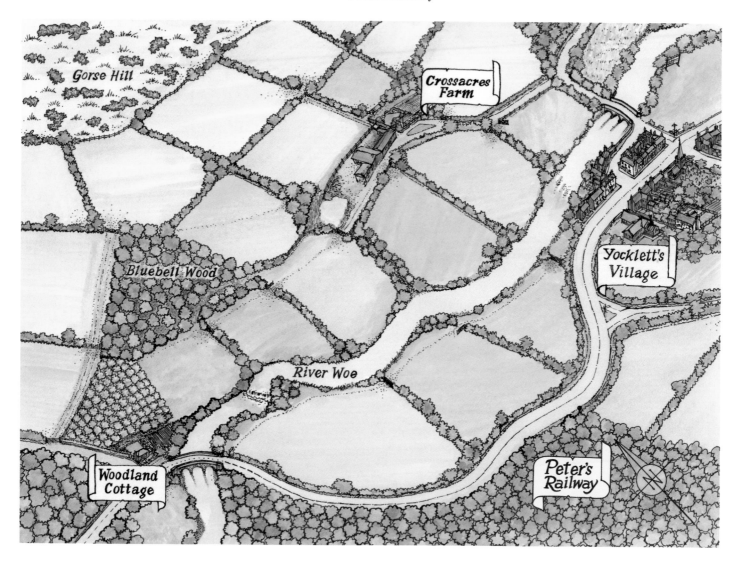

Peter and Grandpa talked about the problem quite often at tea time, while Grandma was reading her newspaper. Peter had suggested making an aeroplane but this seemed to be too complicated for such a short distance and it would use an awful lot of fuel.

"Ah ha," Grandpa said one day, "I've got it! What about a railway? Peter and I could build one across the farm, all the way to Woodland Cottage."

 "Now don't be silly Dear," said Grandma. "It would be much too big, think of all the coal it would use and it would frighten all the sheep. And anyway, what would the neighbours think?"

Grandpa had to admit that she was right. It would be much too big just to go a mile or two, but what else could he do? He thought about the problem while he was working on the farm. He had lots of ideas which were no good, but he kept coming back to the idea of building a railway. Grandma was right though, it would be too big and noisy.

The next week Peter was visiting the farm. He was in the shed chatting with Grandpa while oiling the wheels and mechanism of his go-kart.

"Grandpa," he said, "I've been thinking about your railway idea and how it would be too big."

Grandpa was making something on one of the machines. "Yes," he said. "It was a lovely idea but Grandma is right, it would be much too big and that is the end of it I suppose."

"Well," said Peter, "if a big railway is too big, why don't we build a <u>small</u> railway? We could make it just big enough to carry us, the rest of the family and a few friends. The neighbours would hardly know it was there and the cows and sheep would not be frightened at all."

Grandpa switched off the machine and looked up. A huge smile spread slowly across his face. "Peter my boy," he said, "I think you've got it!"

"It will need to be big enough to carry people," he continued, "but not so big that it takes up a lot of space. I wonder what size it should be?"

"If we make it too small," added Peter, "then we won't be able to fit in the carriages."

"And if we make it too big," said Grandpa, "Grandma will complain and also the materials will be very expensive. I think we will have to go to a railway exhibition and see all the different sizes and then we will know what to do."

The Railway Exhibition

Luckily a few weeks later there was a big railway show and they decided to go. Peter's Dad took them to the station in his car so they could catch the train. Peter had been so excited about the trip that he had hardly slept for several nights before.

When they arrived they could see lots of wonderful models of locomotives and railways in all different sizes. Some were tiny like the ones many children have in their

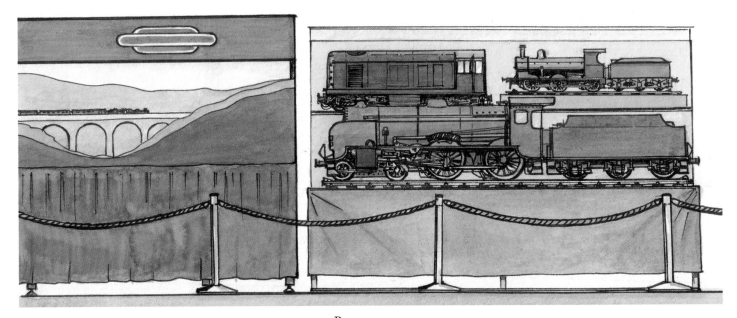

bedrooms. A few were full size, like the train they had travelled to the show in.

One large model in particular caught Peter's attention. The locomotive was called Fiery Fox and was painted in a lovely shade of apple green. It had lots of wheels, a huge boiler and looked very powerful.

"Wow, isn't that a beauty!" said Peter. "I think that is as small as we could make and still be really useful."

The man who had made the model was standing next to it, so they asked him what size or scale it was. "This engine," he replied, "is exactly one eighth of full size. So if something is eight centimetres long on the original, it is one centimetre on the miniature."

Peter asked about the track which it would run on and the man explained. "The gap between the rails, or the gauge of the track, is 7¼ inches (about 18 centimetres) which is just wide enough to make it stable when people are sitting on top of the trucks. If you have track which is any narrower than this, the train will be a bit too wobbly and you might all fall off. You can either make carriages which people sit in," he continued, "or you can make wagons or trucks where they sit on the top."

Peter and Grandpa thought it was very important that it would not be wobbly. They did not want Grandma falling off in the middle of a field of cows.

Grandpa thought he had better tell the man what he was hoping to do. "I am thinking of building a railway across my farm," he explained, "so that my grandson Peter and I and our families can use it to travel between our houses."

"I realise there is an awful lot to do," Grandpa continued. "What with the trucks to make, the locomotive to build and of course the railway itself. It's about a mile long and the journey would be through some pretty countryside with woods and maybe a river to cross….."

Grandpa was just getting into his stride describing what the railway would be like when the man interrupted him. "I tell you what," he said. "If you build a railway as lovely as it sounds across your farm, I will lend you my locomotive to pull the trains. That will get you running much more quickly than if you have to make the engine as well."

"How very kind of you," said Grandpa.

"That's fantastic!" gasped Peter. "Do you really mean it?"

"Well the thing is," the man explained, "I only have a small garden and so I don't have anywhere to run this splendid engine. It took me a long time to make and there is nothing I would like more than to see it running on an exciting railway with something useful to do."

"My name is Mr Esmond," he said introducing himself. "Let's swap addresses and phone numbers, then when you have finished the railway, you can give me a ring and I will bring Fiery Fox over to you."

On the way home in the train, Peter and Grandpa talked excitedly about all the things they would have to do to build the railway. "First of all," started Grandpa, "we will have to survey a route across the farm all the way to Woodland Cottage. We will look for the way with least obstacles, even if it means not going in a straight line. We'll make the railway follow the shape of the land so that the trains do not have to go up and down steep hills."

Peter continued. "We will have to build an engine shed near your workshop and a station at each end of the line."

"And we will need to make a lot of track," said Grandpa. "I think a good job for you Peter, would be to cut up all the wooden sleepers to hold the metal rails."

"Alright," agreed Peter. "That will be my great work for the railway. I shall make every last one of them and then whenever I travel on it, and the sleepers are whizzing by underneath, I will know that I made all of them myself."

"We will have to do a bit of digging to prepare the ground, so that we get a good flat base to lay the track on," explained Grandpa. "And where it's a bit hilly, we may have to dig some cuttings and maybe make some embankments to go over any small hollows. We don't want a railway like a roller coaster!"

Peter thought that a roller coaster railway would be rather good fun but he knew that locomotives did not like pulling heavy trains up and down steep hills.

'I wonder if we will have to build any bridges or tunnels?' thought Peter to himself, imagining the excitement of a bridge over the river. The very idea of rushing through a dark tunnel with the little dot of light at the end getting bigger as you get closer and the smell of smoke, steam and hot oil lingering in the gloomy depths.... Oh it was all just too exciting!

The next day Grandpa decided he would tell Grandma about the great plan. So that afternoon, while having a cup of tea he cleared his throat and very carefully said, "Er -- I have decided to build a small railway to Woodland Cottage. It will only be one eighth the size of a normal one so it will hardly make any noise, it won't frighten the animals and the neighbours won't even notice it is there."

"Yes Dear," said Grandma. "Make sure the seats are comfortable," and she carried on reading her newspaper as if Grandpa told her things like this every day. The truth is that Grandma had heard many of his wonky schemes in the past but he usually forgot about them after a few days. 'This will be the same as all the others,' she thought to herself, going back to the crossword.

If only she knew!..........

Why Railways Don't Have Steep Hills or 'Gradients'

A small locomotive can pull a very heavy train if the line is flat or level
The reason is that the friction of steel wheels rolling on steel rails is very low.

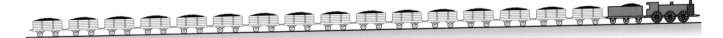

If the hill or 'gradient' is very gentle, the small locomotive can still haul its very heavy train.

If the hill or 'gradient' is too steep, the small locomotive will
only be able to pull a much smaller and lighter train.

Or, to pull the same heavy train, a much larger locomotive will be needed.
This large locomotive will be much more expensive and will use a lot more coal.

Cuttings and Embankments

High ground

What happens when the railway meets a small hill that is too steep to go over?

Or what happens when the railway meets a dip or hollow in the ground that is too steep to go down?

Low ground

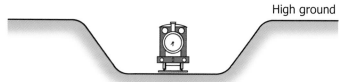

High ground

Cutting
A trench or 'cutting' can be dug through the hill so that the line can go through the hill at the same level

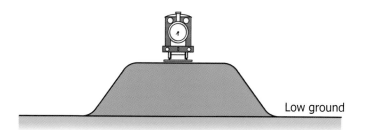

Low ground

Embankment
A mound of earth or 'embankment' can be built up in the hollow so that the line can go across the dipped or hollow area of ground at the same level.

Cutting
through hill

Embankment
over hollow

The railway line runs nice and level through a cutting and over an embankment, even though the ground is hilly and uneven.

Often, and with a bit of luck, the amount of earth needed to make the embankment is the same amount that was dug out of the cutting.

Grandpa's Cunning Plan

Grandpa worked very hard on the farm to get all his jobs and chores finished so that he could spend as much time in his workshop as possible. He was making the carriages and wagons. There was a lot to do: He had to make the wheels, the springs and the bodywork for them. Peter and he had decided that most of the wagons should be like flat trucks so people could sit on top of them.

He also decided to make two of the wagons like the ones used in the old days by the circus to transport their wild animals. One was to be for Cato and the other for Minnie. Cato's wagon would have 'CATO the TIGER' in big letters on the side and Minnie's would have 'MINNIE the JACKAL'. After all Cato was about one eighth the size of a Tiger and Minnie was a Jack Russell and a bit like a mini Jackal, but luckily not so dangerous!

After a while Grandma noticed that it was very quiet around the house and asked, "What are you up to in that shed all the time?"

"Oh, just doing this and that," replied Grandpa, rather mysteriously.

In fact he was getting so excited about building his railway, that he was starting to forget to do some of the other things around the farm. One day Grandma commented, "Today you forgot to feed Minnie and she has eaten all Cato's food. Whatever are you doing all the time?"

"Oh, just building the small railway Dear," he replied. "You know the one -- I told you about it ages ago."

"Gracious me!" exclaimed Grandma. "I thought you had forgotten all about that crazy idea. It will never work and even if it does, you'll never get me to go on it! Not in a hundred years."

'Oh dear', thought Grandpa 'that is a shame. I wonder what I could do to make her change her mind?'

He thought about this a lot and eventually came up with a cunning plan. 'Yes,' he decided, 'I think my plan could work but I'll keep it a secret until opening day and then we'll see......'

Surveying the Route

At the very beginning of the summer holidays, Peter and Grandpa decided to walk between the farm and Woodland Cottage. They wanted to survey a route that would be easy to build the railway on. This meant finding a way which did not have large hills or valleys. It would not be exactly straight but would follow the shape of the land to keep it nice and level. This would make it an interesting journey and, to make it even better, they decided that it should make a small detour to run beside the pond and the river for a little way.

"Now that we have decided on our route," asked Peter, "how can we remember exactly where it goes while we build it?"

Grandpa had already been thinking about this problem. "That's easy," he replied. "We'll bang some wooden stakes into the ground every two or three metres to remind us. Then we can use a spirit level on a long plank of wood to show us what height the track must be, to get it all nice and level. We can bang some more stakes into the ground so that their tops are all level. Then when we are digging out the track bed we can use them to guide us."

Banging in the wooden stakes and getting their tops level took the rest of the weekend. By the time they had finished, it was Sunday evening and getting dark. Peter went to bed tired but contented; at last he could see in his imagination where the trains were going to run.

There was going to be a lot of hard work preparing the ground for the track, but luckily Grandpa had an old digger which he used for odd jobs around the farm. This would make it much easier than digging by hand with a pickaxe and spade.

The next weekend Grandpa went to start up his old digger. With a rumbling noise and a belch of smoke the old diesel engine grunted and then roared into life and work on the track bed could begin.

Peter was on the ground guiding the digger and Grandpa was following his signals. The trench they were digging would exactly follow the route they had marked out with the stakes. "Left a bit!" shouted Peter over the noise of the machine. "Up a little," or, "Down a bit," he would call, to keep the track bed to the correct height.

Metre by metre they dug their way along the route of the railway. Sometimes they needed to dig a much deeper trench to form a cutting where the ground was too high. In other places they had to dump some of the surplus earth to make an embankment. This was to keep the track bed level where the ground dipped away into a hollow.

When they got to the part of the line where the track went through Bluebell Wood, they were lucky because they did not need to cut down any trees. Peter had walked in the woods so often that he knew of a way through where there were enough gaps between the trees to leave room for the line. It would have to be a bit wiggly, with lots of curves, but that was better than cutting down any of the grand old trees.

How a Spirit Level Works

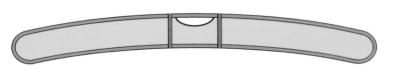

The spirit level is a tool for showing when something is level or flat.

It contains a little glass tube (blue) which is curved.

The glass tube contains a coloured liquid, usually a greenish yellow colour and one small bubble of air.

This bubble always floats to the highest point in the tube. The highest point is in the middle.

There are usually two lines on the tube (red) which show when the bubble is in the centre and therefore shows that the tool is really level.

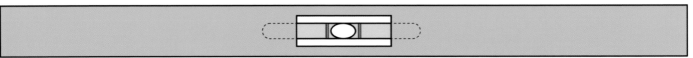

The little glass tube and its bubble are set in a frame which is usually made of wood, metal or plastic (brown). The whole thing or tool is called a 'spirit level'.

To check if a surface is flat or level, the tool is set down on the surface and the bubble observed. If the surface is level then the bubble will be in the middle, between the two lines.

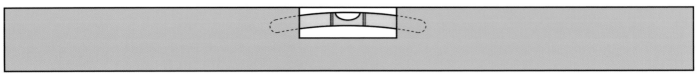

This is the view from above the spirit level. The bubble is clearly seen between the two lines, showing that it is level. (Note that the tube looks straight from above.)

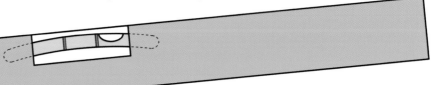

If the spirit level is not flat, or tipped up at one end, the bubble will rise to the highest point in the curved tube and will be off-centre. The bubble always moves to the end which is higher so it is easy to work out how to adjust the surface to make it level.

Setting Out the Track Levels

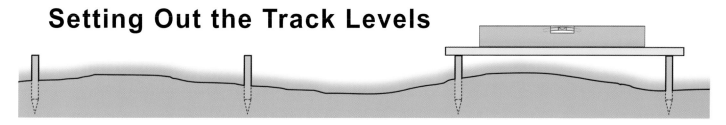

Cross Section of a Grassy Field

In this drawing, stakes (blue) have been driven into the ground and the spirit level is being used to make sure they are all at the same height or level.

The distance between the stakes is greater than the length of the spirit level so a straight plank (yellow) is being used to increase its reach.

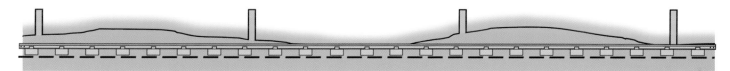

The track bed (dotted black line) has been dug very flat and level by measuring down from the tops of the stakes to the bottom of the track bed as it is being cut out of the ground.

When a bed of small stones or 'ballast' has been put on the track bed and raked smooth, the track can be laid down on top. Some more ballast is then added to go round the sleepers and hold the track in place.

The spirit level can be used, resting on the top of the rails, to make any last adjustments. A bit of ballast is put in under low spots and some ballast is taken out from under high spots.

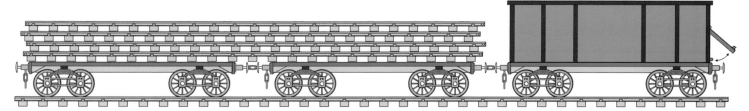

Peter's Track Laying Train

Four lengths of track and a load of ballast can be delivered to the end of the line or 'railhead'. There is a hinged door (red) at the back of the ballast wagon which allows the ballast to be tipped out onto the track bed, ready for raking level.

Making the Track

The next major job was to make the track itself. "Track is quite simple really," said Grandpa. "We will need steel rail for the trains to run on and wooden sleepers to go under the rails, to support them and hold them the correct distance apart. Oh yes, and a few screws to hold the rails to the sleepers."

Then they sat down with a piece of paper and a calculator to work out the quantities of the materials they would need. When they had measured the route of the railway they found it was a little over half a mile or a thousand metres long. Luckily it was quite a lot shorter across the fields than going round by the road. There were two rails so that meant they would need 2000 metres of rail. The sleepers needed to be spaced every 20 centimetres which works out at five sleepers for every metre of track. Tap tap tap went Peter with the calculator, "One thousand times five is er……. Five thousand."

"*Five Thousand sleepers?*" he wondered out aloud. "That seems an awful lot Grandpa."

"Well it will certainly keep you out of mischief for a while Peter," said Grandpa with a grin. "And with four screws to hold the rails to each sleeper we will need twenty thousand screws!!"

Sadly there was no way that Grandpa and Peter could make the steel rails or the screws, so Grandpa had to order these from a factory. They would be delivered in about a month.

However, when it came to the wooden sleepers to hold the rails together they were luckier. While they were digging the track bed through the woods, they had found a huge old oak tree which had blown down in a storm. "Now then," said Grandpa, "if we could cut up that tree into thin strips, they would make the most perfect sleepers for us. And, being oak, they will last forever."

"But Grandpa," said Peter, looking rather doubtful, "making all the sleepers was my job, but I thought I would be cutting them to length from strips of wood. Cutting up a huge tree seems to be much more difficult."

Luckily Grandpa knew a man in a nearby village who owned a saw-mill. He didn't know his name but always called him Mr Plank. Anyway he asked him if he would come and have a look at the oak tree and see if he could cut it up for them.

Mr Plank did some calculations and said, "I reckon that there is plenty of tree to make all your sleepers and there will be quite a lot of it left over. If you let me keep the extra timber to sell as floor boards, then I will cut up your sleepers free of charge. I will even cut them to the correct length for you."

"Thank you very much!" said Peter. "You have no idea how much hard work you will save me. You will be welcome to ride on the train whenever you like."

"With the sleepers all cut to size," explained Grandpa to Peter, "all you will need to do is drill four holes in each one for the screws to hold down the rails. We'll make a little gadget called a jig to help you put the holes in the right place without measuring each one separately. It's ever so simple; just a piece of metal plate with guide holes drilled in it. You place it over the sleeper and the holes guide the drill so that you always drill the screw holes in the right place."

It was not long before two trucks arrived at the farm. One of them had the steel rails in three metre lengths and the other had the sleepers from Mr Plank's saw-mill. "Now we can make a start on building the track," Grandpa told Peter on the telephone that evening. "There is a lot to do, but if we do a bit at a time it will soon be finished."

Peter and Grandpa spent as much time as they could in the workshop making track lengths. Peter drilled all of the holes in the sleepers and Grandpa drilled the holes in the ends of the rails so that they could all be bolted together in a line.

It took a long time, but to help him see how he was getting on, Peter arranged the sleepers in a huge stack. After he had drilled them he then put them on another stack. It was fun to see one stack getting smaller while the finished stack grew and grew.

Finally all of the sleepers and rail ends were drilled and it was time to start assembling the track. Using fifteen sleepers, two rails and sixty screws to hold them down, they could make up a three metre length of track or a *panel*.

As they finished each one, they carried it outside and added it to a growing pile, waiting for the day they could be laid on the track bed to complete the railway.

One evening, looking at the huge pile of track panels, Peter realised that it was going to be a lot of hard work, carrying all the track and other materials to the end of the railway where it would be needed. As they built the railway towards Woodland Cottage they would have even further to carry everything.

"Do you think," he asked Grandpa, "that we could make a wagon to run on the finished part of the line, to carry stuff to the end where we are working?"

Grandpa thought this was a great idea. "In the old days they called the end of the unfinished line the railhead. We'll make one of the wagons specially for moving material and call it the Engineers' Wagon," he decided. "We can push it along and save ourselves a lot of hard work. It will be most useful when we have to take all the ballast along the line."

"What's *ballast* Grandpa?" Peter wanted to know.

"Ballast is the name given to the stones which are put down on the track bed and under the track itself. It makes a really good base for the track because the stones grip the sleepers when they sink in and it lets the rain run away so they don't go rotten. If you look at a full size railway you will see that is exactly what they use to hold the track in place. We will just use smaller stones."

"Well, if it's good enough for the big railways, it's good enough for me," said Peter. "I expect we will need lots of it."

"We will need tons and tons of it," said Grandpa, "but your wagon idea will make light work of moving it along to where we need it. We'll make the wagon with high sides so that it will hold a lot of the ballast and we will make one end open like a door. Then we can let it all out onto the track bed at the end of the line."

The next morning, Grandpa telephoned the quarry and asked them to deliver a lorry load of ballast. It would be dumped near the end of the line where it could be loaded into the Engineers' Wagon.

Track Construction

Viewed from above, the two steel rails (yellow) on which the train runs are held to the correct distance apart or 'gauge' by wooden sleepers (brown).   In this simple form of construction the rails are held down to the sleepers by large screws (red).

There are many different ways of securing the rails to the sleepers, using curly spring clips or metal 'chairs' which the rail sits in.   However the method shown here is the one chosen by Peter and Grandpa for their railway because of its simplicity.

(In America the sleepers are called 'ties')

The distance between the inside of the rails is called the 'gauge' of the track.

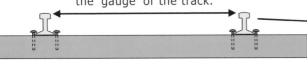

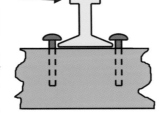

Viewed from the end, it can be seen that the rails have a wide part or 'flange' at the bottom. The large heads of the screws overlap this flange and so hold the rail down onto the sleeper.

The wide area at the top is sometimes called the rail head and is the part the train wheels run on.

The thinner part or 'web' between the head at the top and the flange at the bottom is made thinner to save metal where it is not needed.

Viewed from the side there are two holes drilled in each rail at the end of the length of track.

These holes are used for joining one track section or 'panel' to the next.

Fishplates - Joining Lengths of Track

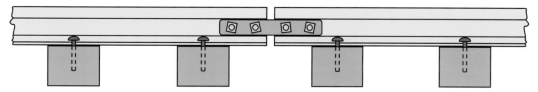

Each length of track or 'panel' is joined to the next by metal fishplates (green) with bolts (pink) through the rails. Usually there are two bolts through the end of each rail. The ones shown here have square heads.

When the track is laid, there is a gap left between the ends of the rails to allow them to expand (get longer) in hot weather when the metal heats up. If they were not allowed room to expand, the track would become buckled and twisted in hot weather and there would be lots of train crashes. These gaps are very important.

It is these gaps between the rails which make the 'tickety-tick' or 'clickety-click' sound as the wheels pass over them.

(Most modern railways use a different method to join the rails which avoids these expansion gaps, however the trackwork in stations is often of the older type shown here.)

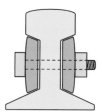

The holes in the fishplates are often oval in shape so that there is room for the bolts to move sideways a little as the rails expand. (Sometimes the holes are round but a bit bigger than the bolts to allow movement.)

The bolts are not done up very tightly so that the rails can slide easily against the fishplates as they expand.

This end view shows a rail, two fishplates, (one either side of the rail) and a bolt.

The two fishplates fit very snugly into the grooves along the side of the rail and hold them very accurately in line.

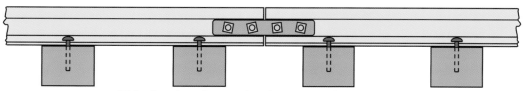

This drawing shows what happens in hot weather.
The rails have expanded and the gap has closed up almost completely.

Constructing the Railway

The next weekend Peter and Grandpa were ready to start laying the track.

The first thing to do was to spread some of the ballast onto the track bed and rake it smooth and level. They did this for some distance and then laid the track panels onto the ballast. When they had set ten panels end to end they bolted them together with nuts, bolts and fishplates.

"Why are they called *fishplates*?" Peter asked.

"That's because on the old railways the plates of metal which bolted either side of the gap between the rails looked a bit like fish," replied Grandpa. "They didn't look much like fish really, but people like to give names to things and *fishplate* is much easier to say than *the bit of metal which bolts the rails together*!"

When several lengths of track had been bolted together they put down more ballast. Now was the time when their Engineers' Wagon would be useful. Peter sat in it and Grandpa pushed him gently along the line and back again. It ran very smoothly with no effort at all.

"Righty Ho! Peter," said Grandpa. "Let's load up some ballast and push it along to the end of our line."

Peter had another idea. "If we couple up two of the flat trucks behind the Engineers' Wagon, we could use them to carry the next length of track. We would save ourselves a journey by taking the ballast and track at the same time."

"That's a brainwave young man," said Grandpa, "we might even put one more flat truck at the back, then one of us can sit on it while the other pushes the train."

So the two of them set to work, loading up the wagon with ballast and the flat trucks with a length of track and then pushing it down the line. One of them would ride and the other push. It was quite easy for Peter to push Grandpa, as the steel wheels rolled very easily on the smooth steel rails and the hills or gradients were very gentle.

When they got to the end of the line or the railhead, it was quite simple: They let the ballast out of the door in the end of the wagon and then raked it smooth and level. After this they lifted the new length of track into place and bolted up the fishplates.

With every trip they made, the line got a little bit longer. It was hard work but the results were easy to see and so they carried on in high spirits, stopping only for meals and cups of tea.

One afternoon when they were having a rest from the hard work, Peter asked, "Grandpa, have you got any good stories about the old railways?"

"Let me see," pondered Grandpa. "Did I ever tell you the true story about the time when a German fighter plane was flying over Kent during the War?"

Peter shook his head, so Grandpa continued.

"Well, he was flying over a small town and there was nothing worthwhile shooting at. But then he saw a train below and decided to take a few pot shots at the locomotive as he flew over."

"Did he hit it?" asked Peter.

"He most certainly did. He hit the boiler and it blew the dome off the top, straight up into the sky with a great whoosh of steam."

"Wow!" said Peter. "Were the engine driver and his fireman hurt?"

"No not at all," said Grandpa, "and by a wonderful fluke, the dome flew up into the air so high and fast that it hit the German plane and brought it crashing down!"

"And what happened to the German pilot?" asked Peter, his eyes wide with excitement.

"Well here is the funny bit, as the story was told to me: He managed to bail out, drifting gently down to the ground with his parachute. Then he walked over to the train which had stopped and said 'Hello' to the driver and fireman."

"The driver of the train said, 'Well you have certainly wrecked our engine Mate!'"

"The German pilot waved over at the remains of his plane, which was now just a smoking heap of twisted metal on the ground, and replied, 'Well you two have certainly wrecked my plane!'" Grandpa chuckled.

"Whatever happened next?" asked Peter.

"They all roared with laughter and sat down and had a cup of tea together from the driver's flask."

"It's a strange thing Peter, but the ordinary people from countries at war would get along just fine. It's the Prime Ministers, Presidents or mad Dictators who set them all against each other."

"Have you got any more good stories?" asked Peter.

"Ah yes," smiled Grandpa with a twinkle in his eye. "I might well have, but I think we had better put down a bit more track first. Otherwise, if I get started on stories about the old railways, we might never finish *our* railway!"

Back to work they went, laying more and more lengths of track, moving the ballast in the wagon and the new piece of track on the two flat trucks behind. Every day they could see the progress they had made and how the line was getting closer and closer to Woodland Cottage.

When Peter wasn't with him, helping on the line, Grandpa would disappear into his workshop where he was making bits and pieces for the railway.

In particular he was working on the two special wagons for Cato and Minnie. They both had a little door in the side and bars to stop the pets falling out when on the move but, at the same time, let in lots of fresh air. He made special water and food bowls which were attached to the floor so that they didn't move about and, one evening when Grandma wasn't looking, he found two old cushions in the house. He put these on the floor of the wagons so that his pets would be quite comfortable.

Peter was so busy building the railway that the summer holiday was flying past. He and Grandpa spent all their time putting down more ballast and track until eventually they reached the garden at Woodland Cottage.

There was a tall and very thick yew hedge all round the garden, but they hoped nobody would mind too much if they cut a hole in it for the trains to go through.

In fact there were several holes or gaps in hedges and fences where the railway crossed from one field to another. Grandpa decided they should make little cattle grids under the track so the animals would not wander through the gaps. These grids have ridges of metal which the animals don't like walking on and would save them from opening and closing gates every time a train went through.

What a sense of achievement they felt as they bolted up the fishplates on the last panel of track. It had been a lot of hard work but at last they could begin to see what the railway would be like when it was finished. It was going to be a most scenic journey.

Flanges
How they keep the train on the track

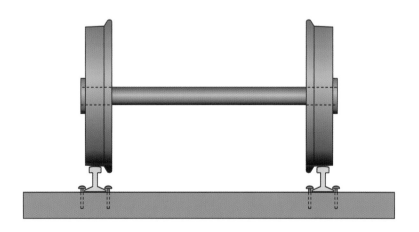

Flanges

Railway wheels are made of steel and have a raised lip or ridge running round the inside edge. This lip is called the flange.

The wheels roll along the steel rails and the flanges keep the wheels central on the track. This means that the train has to follow the track on the straight or around curves.

The driver does not need to steer the locomotive because the track and the flanges do the job for him.

When you consider the vital job that the flanges do, it is amazing how small they are. Next time you travel on a train, look underneath at the wheels and marvel at how such a tiny rim of metal can keep the train from crashing off the rails!

Bogie

A bogie is a truck with four wheels which carry some of the weight of a locomotive, wagon or carriage. (Some bogies for very heavy carriages have six wheels.)

The flanges are clearly visible in this picture and can be seen just inside the rails. They will keep the wheels on the track and steer the train.

The Different Types of Wagons and Trucks

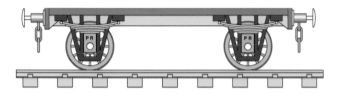

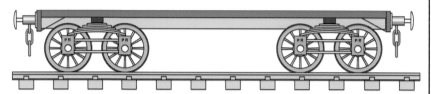

Flat Wagon
A simple type of wagon with four wheels. Used on Peter's railway to carry people and loads

Bogie Flat Wagon
A more complicated wagon with eight wheels on two swivelling bogies. This makes it able to carry much heavier loads and go round tight curves.

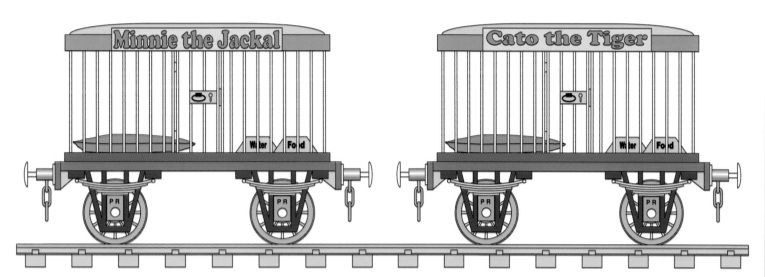

The Dog and Cat Wagons
These two wagons were built to carry Minnie and Cato. They are made in the style of the wagons used by a circus to transport their wild and dangerous animals from one show to the next. In this case the bars are only to stop the pets, who are not dangerous at all, from falling out and hurting themselves.

You can see they each have a cushion for their comfort and also dishes for water and food just in case they get thirsty or hungry on the journey.

Finishing the Line

The line was complete from end to end, but there were still a few things left to do. The biggest of the jobs was to build two little stations and an engine shed to keep the locomotive and trucks safe and dry when not in use. Peter drew some sketches in the evenings to show what he thought would look good.

"They will look fabulous," agreed Grandpa when he had studied the drawings. "And your engine shed will be ideal for raising steam, working on the locomotive when things go wrong, and storing things."

As a natural hoarder, Grandpa kept a pile of handy building materials on the farm, which he could use for various jobs around the place. There was quite a stack of bricks, some roofing materials and bags of cement. And helpfully, when the house had been done up a few years ago, Grandpa had put aside some old windows and doors. In fact, there was everything they needed, just sitting there, waiting for a new use.

They planned to put the engine shed at the end of the garden, next to some old elm trees. After lunch the two railway builders went outside to mark out the ground, to show where the walls would go. Then they used the old digger to dig a trench in the ground to make the foundations.

"Foundations," explained Grandpa to Peter, "are the solid base on which all buildings sit. We'll pour concrete into the trench and after it has set solid, we can build the walls on top of it. That way we know they won't fall over."

The walls were built using bricks and cement, with windows and doors put in as they went. Finally, they put on the roof using wood for a frame and then some metal sheets to make it watertight.

When finished, the engine shed was one long room. It had a low arched door at one end for the train to go in and out. There was space for the locomotive and all the wagons, trucks and carriages; another space for storing coal and shelves for various tools. The windows along one side let in plenty of light so they could see what they were doing. There was also an ordinary door for people to use!

The other thing they installed outside the shed was a water tower to fill the engine's water tanks. The water tower was filled with rainwater from the guttering on the roof of the engine shed and it had a pipe on a swivel. This could be swung out over the engine when it was time to fill up.

The line from the shed ran round behind one of Grandma's flower beds and that is where they decided to put the farm station. They put down some paving stones as a platform and a long bench for passengers to sit on while waiting for a train.

There was a good reason for choosing this particular spot for the station: All good railway stations have an attractive bit of garden with some nice flowers growing. And this was already there and maintained by Grandma!

They also decided to put up a small wooden station building so that they could shelter from the rain, store cushions for the passengers and make cups of tea and coffee.

The station at Woodland Cottage was easier to build because there was already a little wooden play house in the garden. This became the station building and, after laying a few paving stones as a platform, it was finished. There was even an old water butt at the side which collected water from the roof. A short length of hose pipe was all they needed to fill up the locomotive's water tanks.

At long last they were getting close to finishing their railway. The track was laid, the trucks were finished, and they had built the engine shed and stations. All that was left to

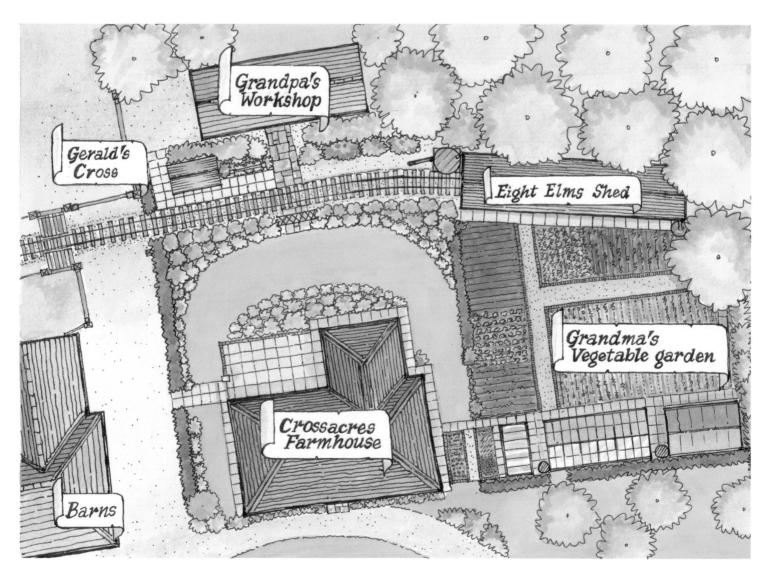

Grandpa's Workshop

Gerald's Cross

Eight Elms Shed

Grandma's Vegetable garden

Crossacres Farmhouse

Barns

make were two sets of buffers to put at the ends of the line so that the train could not run off. They made them in the workshop one evening from some surplus metal rail and, when they were finished, Peter had a suggestion: "Why don't we couple some of the trucks together and push them from one end of the line to the other and back, just to check that everything is perfect?"

Grandpa thought this was a good idea so off they went. It was a long way and they decided that it would be much better when they had a steam locomotive to do the hard work for them. By the time they got back, it was nearly dark.

When they had put everything away, Grandpa and Peter were trying to think of anything they might have forgotten.

Peter was quiet for a moment but suddenly said "We haven't got any names or signs for the stations. What shall we call them?"

"Hum," said Grandpa thoughtfully. "I think I am going to call the station at this end *Gerald's Cross*. What are you going to call your station?"

"Tricky," said Peter, frowning. But then he grinned, "There are lots of Yew trees in the garden at Woodland Cottage, so I am going to call mine *Yewston Station*!" he laughed.

"That's an awful joke," Grandpa chuckled, "but Yewston Station it is. We had better make the signs right away."

Couplings Between Wagons and Engines

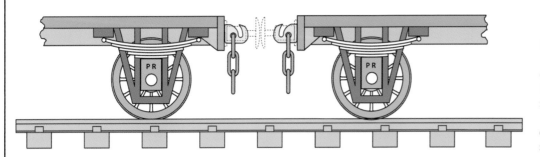

Hook and Chain

Each wagon, carriage or locomotive has a hook and chain at each end.

The hook is shown in yellow and the chain shown in green. The buffers between the vehicles are shown dotted so as not to confuse the drawing.

(More modern types of railway use a different type of coupling which is much safer in a crash)

When two wagons or vehicles need to be coupled together to make up a train, one of the chains is hitched onto the other wagon's hook.

To start with the chain is quite slack so that it is easy for a man to lift it over the hook. Remember that in a full size train, the chain itself will be very heavy.

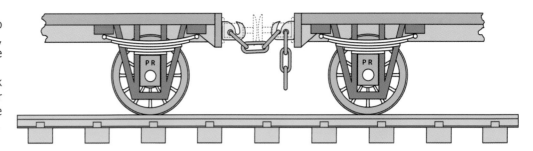

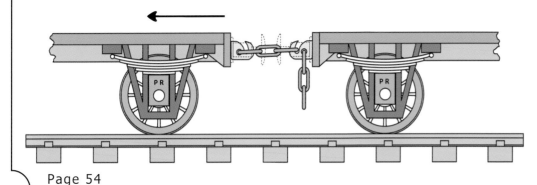

Once a wagon or locomotive starts to pull the next vehicle in the train, the chain is pulled tight.

In this drawing the left hand wagon is pulling on the right hand wagon and the chain has been pulled tight so that it is now straight.

You can see that the buffers (dotted) have now been pulled apart.

Buffers, Chain Couplings and Springs

View from above

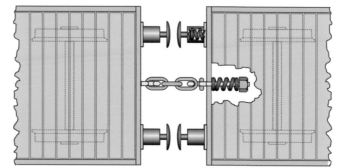

Two wagons are coupled together by a chain and hook. The two pairs of buffers can also be seen. The buffers and hooks have springs (shown in red in cutaway areas) to absorb bumps and bashes.

Buffers

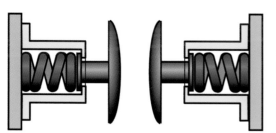

When the train is being shunted, the wagons, coaches and locomotive can bump into each other with a lot of force.

To save them from damage, the springs (red) give a little and allow the buffers to press in a bit, cushioning the impact.

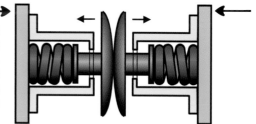

Chain Coupling

When the train starts off, the chain can pull tight with a terrible snatch.

To save the chain from breaking, the springs (red) give a little and allow the hooks (yellow) to pull out a bit instead of the chain being snapped in two.

The buffer beams (purple), which are the ends of the wagons, are pulling away from each other.

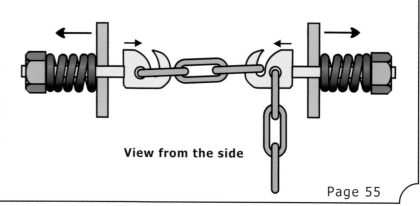

View from the side

Getting Ready to Open the Line

The next day, when they had bolted on the buffers and put up the station signs, Grandpa said, "I think we have finished building our railway, Peter. The only thing left now is to telephone Mr Esmond and ask him to bring over Fiery Fox."

That night Grandpa telephoned Mr Esmond and explained that he and Peter had finished the railway. He asked if the offer to lend them his locomotive was still open.

"My dear chap!" shouted Mr Esmond excitedly. "I am so pleased you rang, and *yes*, I'll bring Fiery Fox over at the weekend. If I come at nine in the morning we'll have plenty of time for me to show you how to drive her. In fact, I can't wait to see her running on a really good line."

"Peter will be so excited when I tell him in the morning," said Grandpa. "We'll organise a Grand Opening Ceremony for the first train from one end of the line to the other."

When he had put down the telephone, he asked Grandma if she could come up with some sort of special tea and cakes for Saturday afternoon. Grandma, always up for a party, agreed straight away. She only needed to know how many to cater for.

They worked it out together. There were the two of them, Peter and his parents and little Kitty and Harry. Mr Plank had been so kind helping with all the sleepers that Grandpa wanted to invite him and his wife. And finally, of course, Mr and Mrs Esmond.

"That's about ten," said Grandma. "I think we should ask Peter if he would like to invite some of his friends as well. If we say two of his friends, that will make twelve and a round dozen sounds like a good party to me. The only thing is, your little train will never pull all those people. "And don't forget," she reminded him, "just because I am cooking a nice tea, don't you go thinking that I'm going to ride on it. I still think it's a crazy idea!"

"Thank you so much for offering to make tea for so many people," replied Grandpa. "I am just sorry that you won't be riding on the train yourself."

Meanwhile he was thinking to himself, 'I wonder if my cunning plan will be cunning enough to make her change her mind?'

The next day was Friday and Grandma spent the whole day baking cakes and other goodies. Grandpa spent the day making final adjustments to the railway, tidying things up and making it all look ship-shape and proper.

The Ceremonial Train would leave Gerald's Cross station at two o'clock and make the first ever trip on Peter's Railway.

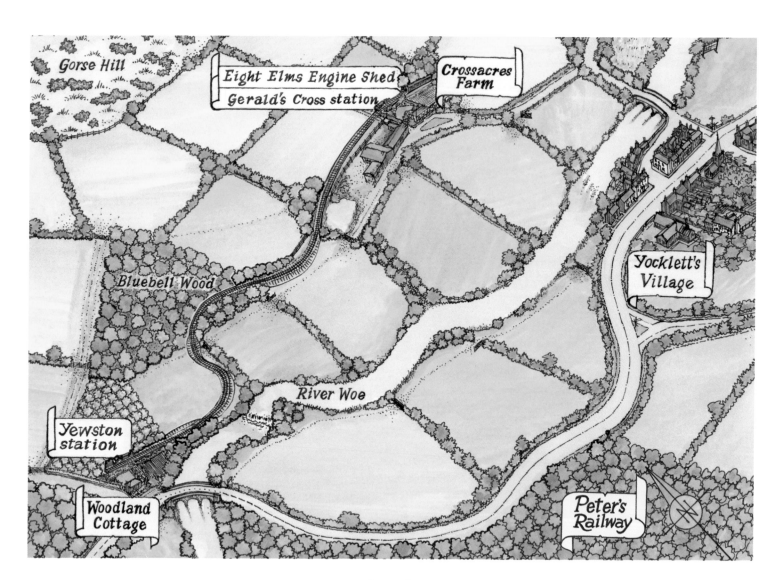

Gorse Hill

Eight Elms Engine Shed

Crossacres Farm

Gerald's Cross station

Bluebell Wood

Yocklett's Village

River Woe

Yewston station

Woodland Cottage

Peter's Railway

Raising Steam

Finally it was Saturday. The great day had arrived.

Mr Esmond appeared with Fiery Fox at nine o'clock on the dot. This gave him plenty of time to show Peter and Grandpa exactly how she worked and all the things they needed to do to drive her correctly.

It was decided that it should be Grandpa who would learn to drive Fiery Fox to start with. One day, when he had got the hang of all her controls and habits, he would then teach Peter to drive.

Fiery Fox was in a large wooden box in the back of Mr Esmond's car and was much too heavy to lift out. They reversed his car up to the end of the line and used a long plank to roll her gently down onto the railway.

With the locomotive sitting on her wheels on the track, they could make a start on the real work of getting her ready to pull the train.

The first job was to fill her boiler with water. This would soon be boiled and turned into steam to drive the engine.

Next they filled her tender with coal and more water to feed into the fire and boiler.

Now for the great moment they had all been waiting for. It was time to light the fire.

First of all Mr Esmond showed them how to put a firelighter and some charcoal in Fiery Fox's firebox. "OK Peter," he said, "you do the honours. Strike a match and light the fire."

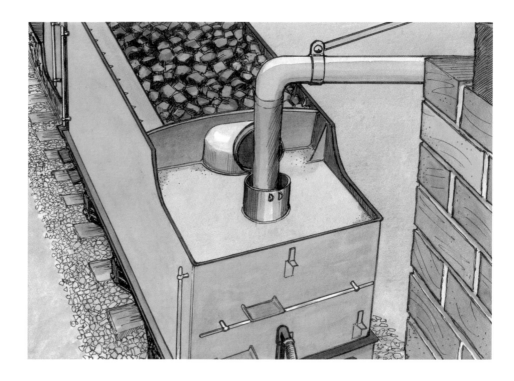

Peter lit the firelighter, which ignited easily, and soon the flames were beginning to set the charcoal alight. Smoke started to curl up from the chimney.

Mr Esmond explained that now the charcoal was lit, Peter could start adding some coal, a little bit at a time so that it wouldn't put the fire out.

Peter shovelled some coal onto the fire and shut the firehole door to keep the heat in and let it get going properly.

"Splendid!" said Mr Esmond. "Now we can relax while we wait for the fire to get going and really hot. You can put a bit more coal on every few minutes, Peter. But now is a good time to oil all the moving parts so that they move smoothly and don't squeak."

Grandpa explained to Peter that they would have to oil her very carefully each time they used her. If they forgot, the moving parts would wear out quickly and they would be most unpopular with Mr Esmond.

Peter said he would make a note of all the different bits as they oiled her this time. Then he would not forget any in the future.

"Thank you Peter, I am sure you will make a most excellent locomotive engineer and driver," said Mr Esmond.

Peter was amazed that there were sixty different moving parts which needed oiling. Luckily some of them were supplied by pipes from little tanks so that filling one tank could oil six different parts.

Once all the little oil tanks and reservoirs were full, Mr Esmond showed them the controls in the cab. The first one was the big red lever on the back of the boiler. "That is the main steam valve or *Regulator*; it controls the flow of steam from the boiler to the pistons and cylinders to make the wheels go round. It is like the accelerator on a car, the more you open it the faster you go."

"This handle is the reverser which controls the valves. You turn it to move the little indicator forwards to set the valves for going forwards and turn it back to set the valves for travelling in reverse. When the indicator is in the middle position the locomotive is safe because, even if you open the regulator, the engine won't start."

"Finally, this handle here is most important; it's for the brakes."

"There are lots of other controls and valves," he said, waving his hand at lots of handles and levers, "but those three are the most important ones for now."

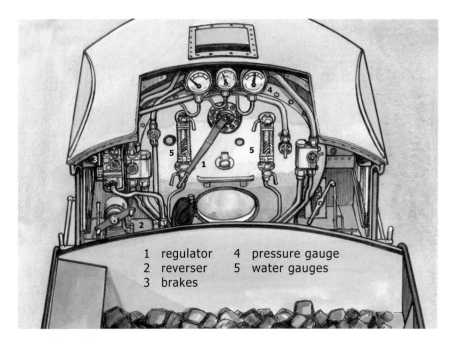

1	regulator	4	pressure gauge
2	reverser	5	water gauges
3	brakes		

While the fire was heating the boiler they could touch the outside and feel it beginning to get warm. At first it was only just possible to feel it, but after about half an hour it was definitely getting quite hot and Peter could only keep his hand on the boiler for a few seconds.

Every few minutes he opened the firehole door and put in a few more shovelfuls of coal. Each time he could see the flames were getting brighter and the fire hotter.

Mr Esmond showed Peter the steam pressure gauge in the cab. "We need it to show a pressure of one hundred to make her work properly," he explained.

"Look," said Peter, "I can see the needle of the pressure gauge has just started to move from the bottom stop. That must mean the water has started to boil and make steam. How much longer will it take to reach working pressure?"

"Only another half an hour," replied Mr Esmond. "This is the best time; just putting a bit of coal on the fire occasionally and plenty of time to chat."

"Grandpa tells great stories about the old days on the railways," said Peter to Mr Esmond. "Do you know any?"

"Well there is one story I could tell you," smiled Mr Esmond, "and now is a good time to tell it because we don't want to have a runaway train!"

"I will tell you a true story, but first we must double check that the steam regulator is turned off and that the brakes are set fully on."

They made sure the regulator was shut, tightened on the handbrake and also checked that the valve gear was in mid-gear or neutral. Then Mr Esmond told his story:

"A long time ago on the London and North Western Railway, very early in the morning, a man lit the fire in an engine called 'Mazeppa'. He had been working on her all night, repairing something, and it was still dark. He needed to light the fire very early because it took such a long time to raise steam in a full size locomotive. When he had got the fire going nicely, he decided to nip off home and go to bed without telling anyone. So off he went and left the engine unattended. What he had forgotten to do was to make sure that the regulator was shut, the valve gear was in mid-position and that the brakes were tightly wound on."

"Now this, Peter, was a most dangerous situation. The fire was getting hotter, the boiler was starting to make steam, the brakes were off, the valves were set in full forward gear *AND* the steam regulator had been left partly open!"

"Good gracious!" said Grandpa. "It was an accident just waiting to happen."

"Yes. No one was watching her, and there wasn't a driver on the footplate. In the darkness, with her steam pressure slowly rising, she started to move. She moved almost silently at first, because the pressure was still low and her chuffs were very quiet. She was slinking through the night like a ghost."

"She ran gently down the lines in the yard and when she got to the gate she smashed through it and out onto the main line."

"No one working in the yard had seen her go and the first anyone knew of the disaster was a man walking to work. He saw her go by on the main line with no one driving. By now her fire was roaring and the steam pressure was high. She was going like the wind!"

"The man ran into the yard to tell everyone what was happening. A driver and fireman jumped on another engine and drove off in hot pursuit of Mazeppa. They never caught up with her though, she was going much too fast. Eventually, after many miles, Mazeppa ran into the back of a train which was stopped in a station. She completely destroyed one of the carriages of the train and some of the passengers were badly hurt."

"What a terrible story," said Peter. "I won't ever forget it and I won't ever forget to make sure the regulator on Fiery Fox is shut when we are raising steam."

"And the brakes and the valves," added Grandpa gently.

Peter wanted to know a bit more about the steam pressure and why the water level was so important. Mr Esmond explained that when water boils in a kettle or a saucepan, there is an opening for the steam to escape so that the pressure never rises. However the boiler for a steam engine is closed and made very strong. When steam is made in a closed boiler, it can't escape. As more and more steam is made it gets squashed in very tightly and the pressure goes up. It is this high pressure which enables the steam to push hard on the pistons of the locomotive and drive the train forwards. The measure used to describe the pressure in most steam engines is 'pounds per square inch' which is usually shortened to psi. This means that at a pressure of 100 psi, the steam is pushing with a force of 100 pounds on every square inch of the boiler or piston.

The water level is very important because as the water boils and is made into steam, the water is used up and its level in the boiler goes down. This can be very dangerous because it is only the water above the metal firebox which stops it from melting: And if the firebox melts, there could be a terrible explosion.

Mr Esmond then showed Peter how to pump water from the tender into the boiler when the water gauge showed that the level was getting low. As you can imagine, they did not have time for lunch. They were much too busy watching the steam pressure and putting more coal on the fire. But most importantly, they were watching the water level in the boiler to make sure it did not get too low and cause an explosion!

"Watching the water level is the most important job Peter and I am trusting it to you," said Mr Esmond.

"There's a lot to remember," replied Peter, "but I won't let you down. I will watch it most carefully."

He looked in the cab and checked the gauges. The water level was correct and then he checked the pressure gauge. "Look!" he shouted. "The steam pressure has got to one hundred pounds per square inch."

The locomotive was oiled, the fire was hot and at last they had steam up.

They were *ready*.....

The Boiler - How the Locomotive Makes Its Steam

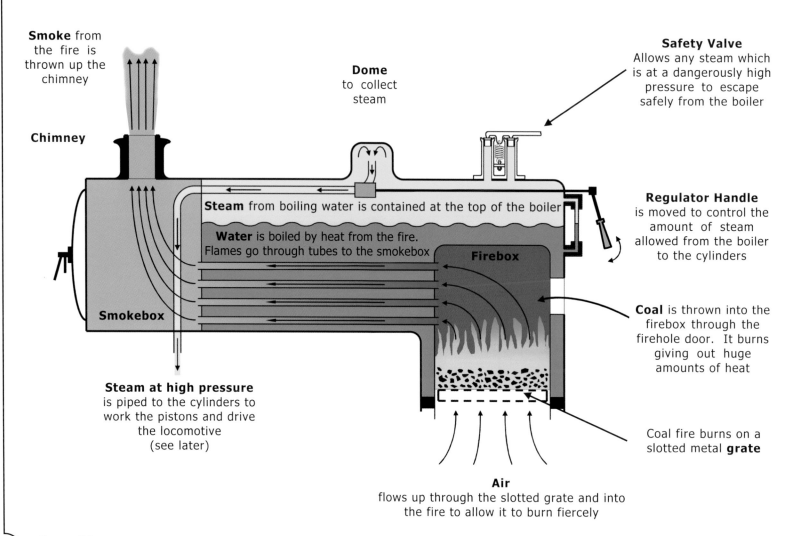

Smoke from the fire is thrown up the chimney

Chimney

Dome to collect steam

Safety Valve Allows any steam which is at a dangerously high pressure to escape safely from the boiler

Steam from boiling water is contained at the top of the boiler

Water is boiled by heat from the fire. Flames go through tubes to the smokebox

Firebox

Smokebox

Regulator Handle is moved to control the amount of steam allowed from the boiler to the cylinders

Coal is thrown into the firebox through the firehole door. It burns giving out huge amounts of heat

Steam at high pressure is piped to the cylinders to work the pistons and drive the locomotive (see later)

Coal fire burns on a slotted metal **grate**

Air flows up through the slotted grate and into the fire to allow it to burn fiercely

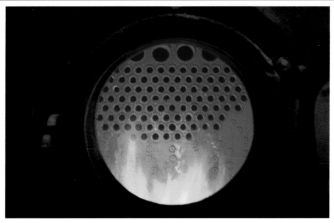

Firebox

This is a view into the firebox of a locomotive when the fire is burning. You can see the flames and the ends of the tubes which carry the fire to the smokebox. (The tubes are sometimes called 'fire tubes'.)

The tubes go through the water in the boiler and the flames in the tubes heat the water and turn it into steam.

Fire Tubes
This photograph catches some flames disappearing into the fire tubes.

Smokebox

This is a view of the smokebox of an old engine, found in a shed in Argentina. The smokebox door is missing so you can see inside. The fire tubes are clearly visible.

When the engine is running, the smoke from the fire and flames comes out of the tubes and up the chimney. (You can see the chimney behind the large lamp.)

The Grand Opening Ceremony

It was ten to two in the afternoon and time to get ready for the inaugural train.

They pulled out the wagons from the engine shed and coupled them up behind Fiery Fox. It was a long train and made quite a sight.

Grandpa sat on the seat on Fiery Fox's tender and very carefully drove the engine and train along the new line and round to the station platform by Grandma's garden. Smoke and steam were coming out of the chimney as they glided slowly along the track with the locomotive chuffing quietly. Mr Esmond was riding on one of the wagons and Peter was riding on the last one.

Everyone was waiting for them at the station. There was Grandma, Peter's Mum and Dad, Jo and Colin, the little twins, Kitty and Harry and two young friends, William and Stella. There was Mrs Esmond and also Mr and Mrs Plank and we mustn't forget Minnie and Cato. They were standing on the platform wondering what on earth was going on. Quite a crowd!

Peter gently put the dog and cat into their special wagons. They didn't look much like scale sized jackals and tigers but they didn't seem to mind. And, what with the old cushions and food, they didn't even notice when he shut the doors to keep them safe.

Everyone got onto the train except Grandma, who was still standing on the platform. "Well everybody, I hope you have a lovely trip," she announced, "but I am afraid I won't be coming with you."

"Oh come on Grandma!" they all shouted. "Don't worry, you'll be just fine."

But Grandma was not so easily moved. She had made up her mind. "No. It's not for me, it looks far too uncomfortable."

Just then, Grandpa went to Peter and whispered in his ear. "You keep an eye on things for a moment. There is something I have to do."

He went off up the track towards the engine shed and a few minutes later came back pushing something down the line. It was hidden under a blanket and everyone was wondering what it could be. He coupled it up to the rear end of the train.

"Grandma," he called. "Could you come over here for a minute?"

"Whatever have you got under there?" she asked.

Grandpa pulled the blanket off with a great flourish and revealed a splendid saloon carriage. Painted a vibrant green with red edges, it had a roof, sides and a door. Inside was a proper comfortable seat with nice padding and cushions. And on the side in big gold letters it said 'G.W.'

Grandpa leant over and whispered in Peter's ear, "Don't tell Grandma, but G.W. stands for Granny Wagon!"

"Well? What do you think?" he asked Grandma. "I made it especially for you. I hope that you will like it so much that you will change your mind and travel on Peter's Railway."

"You made all this just for me?" she asked, shaking her head in amazement.

"Yes Dear, and look inside: It even has an oil lamp in case it gets dark. You could read the paper as we steam along the line."

Grandma's Special Saloon Carriage

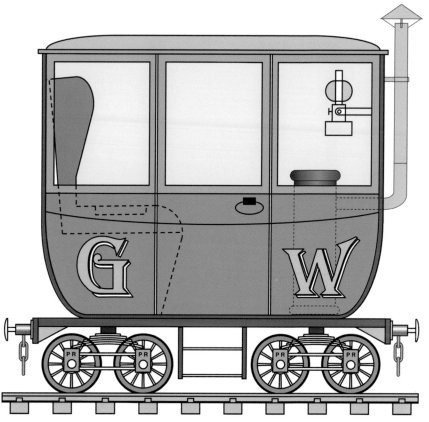

The Granny Wagon

This is the luxurious 'saloon carriage' which Grandpa constructed to persuade Grandma to ride on the railway. He made it as grand and comfortable as possible so that she would find it difficult to refuse to go in it.

He made it with a strong body complete with door and windows, to make Grandma feel very safe and to keep out the draughts.

Included in the fittings are an upholstered armchair and an oil lamp in case she wants to read or do the crossword during a night time trip. And finally, the very height of luxury, he installed a log burning stove to keep her warm in cold weather. (They are burning off-cuts of wood from when they made all the sleepers and have enough to last for many years.)

"Well I never!" she said. "I suppose I had better have a good look at it, seeing as how you have gone to all this trouble."

She looked all over the carriage and then inside. "You must have spent an awful lot of time making it. There's even a log burning stove to keep me warm."

"Yes," said Grandpa, "I wanted it to be so nice that you would be happy to ride in it. I've even lit the stove for you to give it a warm welcoming glow."

"And look," said Grandma, "it says 'G.W.' on the side. That must stand for *'Great Western'*. Now that was the safest railway there ever was."

Peter and Grandpa winked at each other. They wouldn't tell her what it really meant.

"Oh well," she said at last. "With all the work you've put into it, and all just for me, it would be a terrible shame not to at least give it a go." And without any more delay she climbed in, sat down and pulled the door shut with a clunk.

Finally they coupled up the guard's van behind Grandma's carriage for Peter to ride on. He was the guard of the train and it was his job to ride at the back so he could see that all was well.

The great moment had arrived.

Everyone was on the train.

Grandpa was at the controls.

It was two o'clock.

Peter blew a whistle.

Grandpa let off a long blast on Fiery Fox's steam whistle and slowly opened the regulator.

Fiery Fox moved forward as the steam pushed on her pistons. She broke through the ribbon which Peter had tied across the track.

Everyone on the train let out a loud cheer and they slid slowly out of Gerald's Cross station with Fiery Fox chuffing in a most business-like way.

It was a lovely trip with everyone enjoying the sights and smells of the farm as they rolled along. After running through the garden and past the house, the railway went through a hole in the hedge and into the yard. They skirted around the edge of the duck pond and dived through a hole in another hedge into the front field.

This was a large meadow where Grandpa's lovely Highland cattle were quietly munching away. When the train appeared through the hedge, some of them ran away, some of them ran towards it to see what was happening and others carried on chewing the cud as if a small steam train ran through their field every day.

The railway ran along the edge of the field for quite some distance until, at the far side, it reached a gap in the fence and disappeared into Bluebell Wood. It was very pretty going through the wood and the train wound its way through the trees in a very curvy route. Grandpa had to slow down a bit, but everyone enjoyed it because there was something different to see after each bend.

Suddenly they shot out of the dappled half light of the woods into the bright sunshine again. They were crossing a grass field with sheep in it. The railway had been a bit more difficult to construct across this field because it wasn't very flat. They had kept the line nice and level by digging some cuttings through the high bits and using the earth they dug out to make embankments over the dips. Going through the cuttings was exciting because the sides seemed to rush past the passengers and the view from the top of the embankments was tremendous.

After crossing the field the railway ran alongside the river for a while. This was one of the prettiest parts of the journey. There was the River Woe and its waterfalls to look at, also the trees along the edge and all of the other things which make a river so attractive.

The journey was coming to an end as the railway turned away from the riverbank and along the edge of a large orchard of apple trees. It took quite a long time to cross the orchard but at the end was the hedge at the bottom of Woodland Cottage garden.

Grandpa shut off steam so the train would start to slow down. He didn't want to overshoot the end of the line, hit the buffers and end up in a flower bed. The train was so heavy that, at first, it seemed to carry on without slowing down at all. But at last it began to lose speed as they went though the hedge and into the garden. Just a slight touch on the brakes and the train pulled up at the platform, right next to Peter's little playhouse, now proudly named 'Yewston Station'.

Everyone got off the train and they were all talking at once about what a splendid railway it was, what a lovely view you get from the train - so much better than going by car and so on.

Grandma got out of her saloon carriage beaming with smiles. "That was wonderful," she laughed, "I can't think what I was worried about. I am looking forward to the return trip already."

Grandpa and Peter had not yet built a turntable at either end of the line. This meant that for the return trip they would have to reverse the whole train, with the locomotive running backwards and pushing the train from the rear. It didn't really matter for now, Fiery Fox would run just as well backwards as forwards. Peter would just have to keep a good lookout from the guards van, now at the front of the train. He would blow his whistle to alert Grandpa at the back if there was anything on the track. It wouldn't do to run over a cow, it might wreck the train!

Building the turntables could be one of their next projects….

After everyone had made suitably good comments about the garden at Woodland Cottage, it was time to get back on the train for the return trip to the farm and the grand tea which Grandma had laid out.

Peter blew the whistle, Grandpa answered with a toot on the steam whistle and slowly reversed the long train back up the line.

On arrival back at Gerald's Cross it was time for tea. Grandma had made a special cake to celebrate the opening of the railway and Peter and Grandpa held a large knife together and cut it up.

Everyone cheered again and Grandpa thanked Grandma for the splendid tea and then announced in a loud voice: "I now declare Peter's Railway well and truly open!"

After tea they spent the rest of the afternoon travelling back and forwards on the train, picking people up and dropping them off. Between trips they filled themselves up with food and drinks and the locomotive with coal and water.

On one trip they found Minnie the dog running along behind the train chasing it. She was barking and wagging her tail, enjoying every minute. After a while, when the train went into the wood, Minnie disappeared and Peter thought that she had been left behind because they were going too fast for her.

However when they arrived at Yewston station, Peter and Grandpa were amazed to find Minnie standing on the platform, waiting for them. She was wagging her tail excitedly and barking a welcome. The train had not been too fast for her at all, she had overtaken it in the woods.

When they had finished making a fuss of her, Grandpa said, "Now that reminds me of a story from the very earliest days of the railways."

"There was a railway in Cumbria," he started, "and a farmer was travelling in one of the carriages with his dog. He was only going one stop but before the train set off, the guard came through to check the tickets. Well he had a right old argument with the farmer because he said that dogs did not travel free and the farmer would have to buy it a ticket."

"The farmer was furious and refused to buy an extra ticket, so the guard said the dog would be put off the train. With that, the farmer took his dog and tied it to the back of the train with a piece of string and got back in and sat down."

"This made the guard angry. He felt that the railway was being cheated so he told the engine driver to go as fast as he could."

"Now Peter, you might think the farmer was being very cruel and that the dog would be killed by being dragged along by a train. But when they got to the next station the dog was already standing on the platform, wagging its tail and barking. It had broken the string and overtaken the train, just like Minnie. Locomotives, you have to remember, did not go very fast in the old days and the dog had enjoyed a bit of exercise and the new sport of racing trains!"

Peter thought this was a great story and gave Minnie another well deserved pat on the back.

They spent the rest of the afternoon and evening running trains until finally it was too dark to carry on.

They put the train back into the shed and let Fiery Fox's fire die down and go out.

While they were cleaning all her paintwork and brass, they thanked Mr Esmond for lending them his locomotive.

Mr Esmond said he was delighted. "You have made a truly splendid railway and it was a real pleasure to see her working so well, pulling such a long train and being such a useful engine. You can borrow her for as long as you like and I shall look forward to coming to visit from time to time."

After a bit more chatter, it was time to close the shed door for the night and for Mr and Mrs Esmond to go home. They set off down the farm road in their car, waving good bye.

It was also time for Peter to go home and to bed. He was tired but very happy. "Thank you Grandpa for building the railway with me," he said.

"I enjoyed it," replied Grandpa, "and anyway it was all your idea. Just remember not to tell Grandma what 'G.W.' really stands for. She would never go in her carriage again if she knew."

That night Peter dreamt of travelling back and forwards on his railway and learning to drive Fiery Fox.

But that is another story....

The End.

Pistons and Cylinders
How the steam turns the wheels and drives the locomotive

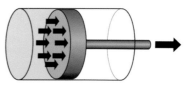

Steam presses on a round piston which is a close sliding fit in the cylinder (a round tube).

The piston and its rod push on the connecting rod which pushes the wheels round. The connecting rod turns the wheels by pushing on a crank, just like a bicycle pedal.

The steam comes from the boiler and is at very high pressure so that it pushes the piston with great force. This is why steam locomotives are so powerful.

Follow the numbered pictures to see how it works:-

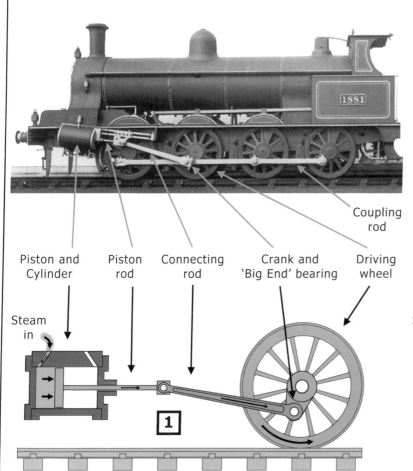

Coupling rod

| Piston and Cylinder | Piston rod | Connecting rod | Crank and 'Big End' bearing | Driving wheel |

Steam is let into the left end of the cylinder and pushes the piston to the right, turning the wheel.

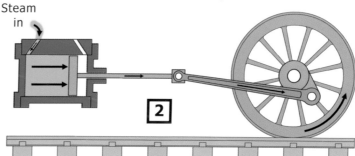

Steam in

Steam in

1

2

Now steam is let into the other end of the cylinder and pushes the piston to the left. The piston is now pulling the connecting rod to pull the wheel round in the same direction.

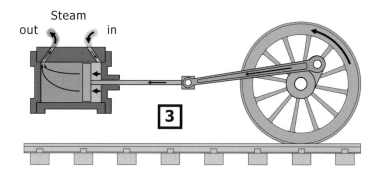

The first lot of steam (now shown in blue) is being let out of the cylinder to go up the chimney as exhaust steam. The steam is let in and out of both ends of the cylinder by a special valve and mechanism.

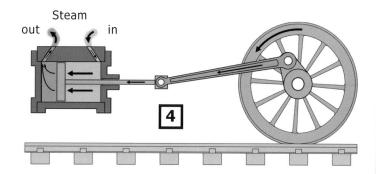

To keep the wheel turning, steam is now let into the left hand end of the cylinder again and the piston keeps turning the wheel the same way.
Again the last lot of steam (now shown in blue) is being let out to go up the chimney.

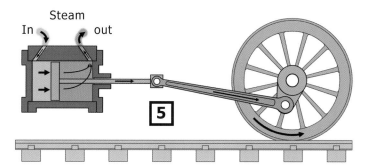

The piston pushes and pulls the wheel round and the cycle of pushing and pulling is repeated as long as the driver wants to keep the train moving.
Every time steam is let out of the cylinder to go up the chimney it makes the chuffing noise which is so well known.

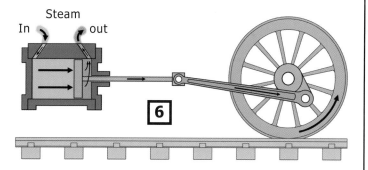

Bongo

Bongo is a miniature steam locomotive, one eighth full size and was made over a period of eight years by Chris Vine. It is a model of an LNER B1, of which 410 were built between 1942 and 1952. (LNER - London North Eastern Railway.)

The original engines weighed 123 tons with the tender and the miniature weighs a little over a quarter of a ton. This is still heavy enough to cause trouble when taking it to exhibitions around the country. The length over the buffers is 8 feet or 2.5 metres.

The B1s were often called the Antelope class because many of them were named after different types of deer: Springbok, Impala, Gnu, Wildebeeste, Gazelle and many more. No. 8306 was named Bongo (a particularly attractive African antelope, chestnut red with white stripes) and from then on they were all known as the Bongos.

It was made in a shed in the author's garden using a lathe, drill and milling machine and many other small hand tools. It is not made from a kit; almost all the parts were made from bars, strips and sheets of metal. The similarity between Fiery Fox and Bongo is no coincidence!

Chris has not yet discovered the top speed, but has frightened himself a few times. About 15 mph has been achieved (a scale speed of 120 mph) and Bongo was still accelerating alarmingly......

The Author at Speed

Some Special Words

Ballast	Rough stones which are put under the track to hold it in place.
Bogie	Four (or six) wheeled truck under a large carriage or wagon to spread out the load on the track.
Boiler	The part of the locomotive where water is boiled to make the steam.
Connecting rod	Connects the piston to the crank to turn the wheels.
Crank	Like a pedal on a bicycle. It converts a push-pull motion to a rotating motion.
Cutting	Trench dug through a high piece of ground to keep the line level.
Cylinder	Round and smooth tube which contains the piston. The cylinders and pistons are the parts of the locomotive where the power in the steam is converted into the useful motion of the train.
Drilling machine	Machine for turning drills to make round holes in wood and metal.
Embankment	Built up mound of earth which carries the line over a dip in the ground.
Firebox	The metal box which contains the fire. It is completely surrounded by water.
Fishplate	Metal plate used to join rails together.
Gauge (of track)	The distance between the two rails.
Gradient	Slope or hill. Usually on railways they are fairly gentle compared to roads.
Jig	Simple device to make repetitive tasks easier when making things.
Lathe	Machine tool for making parts which are mainly round - e.g. Wheels.
Milling machine	Machine tool for making parts which are mainly flat - e.g. Connecting rods.
Panel	Length of assembled track with rails attached to the sleepers.
Piston	Round disk which fits perfectly and slides in the cylinder. Steam pushes on the piston to turn the wheels by using the connecting rod and crank.

Pressure	When a lot of steam is squashed into a closed space, its pressure rises.
	Pressure is often measured in 'pounds per square inch' (or 'psi' for short).
	A pressure of 100 pounds per square inch means that on every square inch of the boiler shell or piston, the steam is pressing with a force of 100 pounds.
	A square inch is about 6 square centimetres and 100 pounds is about 40 kilograms or probably the weight of a young person.
	The metric or proper unit of pressure is the 'newton per square metre' or 'pascal'. 100,000 pascals is called 1 'bar' and 1 bar is equal to about 15 psi in old units.
Pressure gauge	Device in the locomotive cab which shows the steam pressure in the boiler.
Regulator	Main steam valve used by the driver to control how much steam is used in the cylinders. The more the regulator is opened, the harder and faster the locomotive works. (The regulator is often called the 'throttle' in America.)
Sleepers	Cross beams which hold the metal rails to the correct gauge or distance apart.
Spirit level	Tool for showing when a surface is level.
Stack	Or smoke stack. The American name for the chimney.
Steam	When water boils it bubbles and turns into steam. Normally steam has a huge volume compared to the water it came from. However in the boiler it is contained in a closed space and so instead of expanding to a large volume, it rises in pressure.
Tender	Large locomotives have a tender behind them to carry supplies of coal and water.
Ties	The American name for sleepers.
Track bed	The formation on the ground which carries the track.
Turntable	Turns a locomotive round so that it faces the other way for a return journey.
Water gauge	Device in the locomotive cab which shows the water level in the boiler.

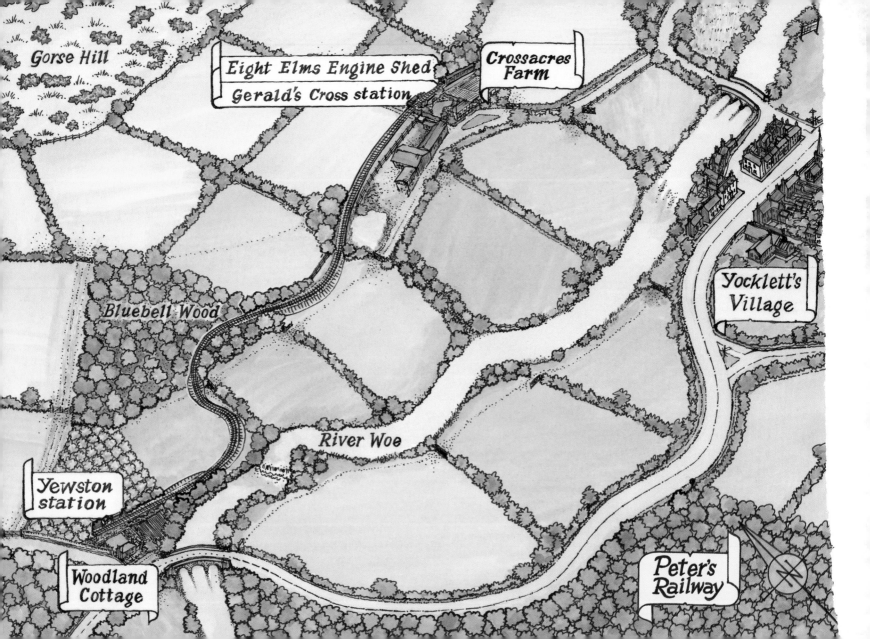

Gorse Hill

Eight Elms Engine Shed
Gerald's Cross station

Crossacres
Farm

Yocklett's
Village

Bluebell Wood

River Woe

Yewston
station

Woodland
Cottage

Peter's
Railway